Franklin Forgets

From an episode of the animated TV series *Franklin* produced by Nelvana Limited, Neurones France s.a.r.l. and Neurones Luxembourg S.A.

Based on the *Franklin* books by Paulette Bourgeois and Brenda Clark.

TV tie-in adaptation written by Sharon Jennings and illustrated by Sean Jeffrey, Mark Koren, Alice Sinkner, and Jelena Sisic.

Based on the TV episode *Franklin Takes the Blame*, written by Nicola Barton.

Franklin is a trade mark of Kids Can Press Ltd.
Kids Can Press is a Nelvana company.
The character Franklin was created by Paulette Bourgeois and Brenda Clark.

ISBN 0-439-08368-0

12 11 10 9 8 7 6 5 4 3 2 1   0 1 2 3 4 5/0

Printed in the U.S.A.   23
First Scholastic printing, May 2000

Franklin Forgets

Based on characters created by
Paulette Bourgeois and Brenda Clark

SCHOLASTIC INC.

New York   Toronto   London   Auckland   Sydney
Mexico City   New Delhi   Hong Kong

FRANKLIN fed his goldfish every day and tidied his room once a week. He helped his parents rake leaves in the fall and shovel snow in the winter. Franklin liked doing chores. It made him feel very grown-up.

One day, Franklin and his friends were putting the finishing touches on their go-cart. Mr. Mole stopped to admire their work.

"All you need is a horn," he said. "Maybe I'll discover the perfect one on my travels."

"Are you going away?" asked Franklin.

"Just for four days," answered Mr. Mole. "First I have to find someone to do a few chores for me while I'm gone."

"I could do your chores, Mr. Mole," Franklin offered eagerly.

"Thank you, Franklin," replied Mr. Mole. "But it's a big responsibility. I think I need someone a little more grown-up."

"But I'm more grown-up than I used to be," insisted Franklin. "And I do lots of chores at home."

Mr. Mole looked at Franklin thoughtfully.

"All right," he agreed. "You've got the job."

Franklin smiled proudly.

That afternoon, Franklin went to Mr. Mole's house to get his instructions. He had three things to remember — collect the mail, fill the birdbath, and water the garden.

"And that's *every* day," Mr. Mole reminded him.

Franklin nodded. "I won't forget," he replied.

Early the next morning, Franklin collected Mr. Mole's mail and filled the birdbath. He was about to water the garden when Bear and Beaver came along.

"Do you want to fly kites with us?" asked Bear.

"I can't," answered Franklin. "I have to water these flowers."

"Can't you do it later?" asked Beaver.

Franklin thought for a minute.

"Okay," he said finally. "I'll do it this afternoon."

Franklin ran home for his kite.

It wasn't until suppertime that Franklin
remembered the garden.

"I'll water it first thing tomorrow," he decided.

But the next morning, Franklin noticed that the
sky was dark and cloudy.

"Hmmm," thought Franklin. "It looks like the
rain will water Mr. Mole's flowers for me."

Franklin was wrong. The sky cleared up, the sun shone bright and hot . . . and Franklin spent the day swimming. He didn't remember his chores until bedtime.

"I won't forget tomorrow," Franklin declared.

But in the morning, Franklin was too excited about his baseball game to think of anything else. After winning, he and Beaver were so busy celebrating that Franklin forgot again. Then he saw his mother mailing a letter.

"Oh, no!" cried Franklin. "My chores!"

Franklin and Beaver rushed to Mr. Mole's.

Franklin's heart sank when he saw Mr. Mole's yard. The birdbath was empty, and the mailbox was full. The flowers lay wilted on the hard, dry earth.

Franklin collected the mail and filled the birdbath, but he didn't know what to do about the flowers.

"Maybe they'll perk up if you give them lots of water," suggested Beaver.

"Good idea!" said Franklin. "I'll let the hose run all night."

The next morning, Franklin and Beaver discovered that things had gone from bad to worse. The garden was flooded, and the flowers were ruined.

Franklin hurried to turn off the hose.

"What are you going to do?" asked Beaver.

Franklin thought hard.

"Maybe I could plant the paper flowers I made at camp," he said. "They might look real."

Franklin raced home to get his flowers. He and
Beaver planted them, row upon row, in the soggy ground.
"How does it look?" asked Franklin.
"Like a bunch of paper flowers stuck in a mud pie,"
answered Beaver.
Franklin felt like crying. The garden looked terrible,
and Mr. Mole was coming home that afternoon.

Franklin couldn't stop thinking about the garden all morning. After lunch, he waited anxiously by Mr. Mole's gate.

At last, Franklin saw Mr. Mole coming down the road.

Franklin's tummy flip-flopped.

"Hello, Franklin," said Mr. Mole. He reached
into his bag and pulled out a shiny new horn.
"I didn't forget," he said cheerfully.
"But I did," Franklin said in a shaky voice.
"I forgot to water your garden. Now it's ruined.
I . . . I'm sorry."
"Now, now, Franklin," said Mr. Mole. "I'm sure
things can't be *that* bad."
Then he opened his gate and gasped.

"It's all my fault, Mr. Mole," Franklin said sadly. "You were right. I'm not grown-up enough."

"Well, the garden *is* a bit of a mess," said Mr. Mole. "But it took a lot of courage to tell me the truth. Taking responsibility for a mistake is a very grown-up thing to do."

"If I help you plant new flowers, would that be grown-up, too?" Franklin asked hopefully.

Mr. Mole smiled. "It sure would," he said.

Before long, Mr. Mole's garden was growing again.

"You know, Franklin," said Mr. Mole, "with all your help, my garden looks better than ever."

"Well," Franklin replied, "I *do* have two green thumbs!"